Dec., 2004

Merry Christmas
Natalie

w/ Love from
Auntie Rosalie &
Uncle Kenny
xx oo

Little Lost Donkey

Dandi Daley Mackall

ILLUSTRATED BY

Elena Kucharik

Tommy
NELSON®

www.tommynelson.com

A Division of Thomas Nelson, Inc.
www.ThomasNelson.com

Published in Nashville, Tennessee, by Tommy Nelson®,
a division of Thomas Nelson, Inc.

Library of Congress Cataloging-in-Publication Data

Mackall, Dandi Daley.
    Little lost donkey / Dandi Daley Mackall; illustrated by Elena Kucharik.
        p. cm. – (I'm not afraid)
    Summary: The donkey chosen to carry Mary to Bethlehem is afraid he
will get lost, but after praying he not only reaches Bethlehem, he finds a
stable where Jesus can be born.
    ISBN 0-8499-7752-5
    [1. Donkeys—Fiction. 2. Jesus Christ—Nativity—Fiction. 3. Fear—Fiction.
4. Prayer—Fiction. 5. Stories in rhyme.] I. Kucharik, Elena ill. II. Title.
PZ8.3.M179 Li 2001
[E]—dc21

                                                                2001042763

· Printed in Singapore
03 04 05 TWP 5 4 3 2

Come listen to my story,
Although you know it well.
For I'm the donkey Mary rode,
And I've a tale to tell.

I overheard one starry night
When Joseph told his bride,
"We have to go to Bethlehem!"
They asked me for a ride.

"I'm sorry, Mary. If I could
I'd take you right away
But I'm afraid you'll end up lost
And never find your way."

"I wonder, might you take a horse?
  Or could you ride that cow?
  Your neighbor has a camel.
  You should go and ask him now."

"But I want you," said Mary,
  As she scratched behind my ear.
"I'm carrying the Son of God;
  So, Donkey, never fear."

Before I knew what happened,
We had set out on the trail.
I don't know where I am! I thought
And shook from head to tail.

I felt young Mary on my back.
The night grew dark and drear.
Clip, clop, my hooves beat out the sound
Upon a midnight clear.

The road grew rough. "We're lost!" I cried.
"I knew I'd lose my way.
I warned you not to count on me."
Then Mary whispered, "Pray."

When I looked up, I knew deep down
The way stretched straight ahead.
I trotted on to Bethlehem.
"We made it!" Mary said.

The city filled with travelers.
The inns were crowded too.
"They're out of rooms!" poor Joseph cried.
"Now what are we to do?"

I led them to a stable bare,
For God showed us the way—
And in a manger Christ was born
On that first Christmas Day.

So if you're lost, don't be afraid.
And don't forget to pray.
Remember Mary's donkey,
And you're sure to find your way.